Pirate Ship Makeover

Written by Quentin Flynn
Illustrated by Bettina Guthridge

Contents

1 Hoist the Mizzen! **4**
2 The Bad Ship *Charybdis* **9**
3 Before and After! **18**
4 Ooh-Arrgh, Ooh-Arrgh **24**
5 The *Charybdis* Transformed **30**
6 All Hands on Deck! **36**

NELSON
CENGAGE Learning
For learning solutions, visit **cengage.com.au**

Meet the Characters

Captain Grizzlethorpe

The captain of the pirate ship *Charybdis*.

Soupy Slickback

A famous TV-show host.

Flotsam

The first mate of the pirate ship *Charybdis*.

Jawbones

The second mate of the pirate ship *Charybdis*.

The *Charybdis*

A pirate ship that has seen better days.

Dear Reader

Here's another story featuring Soupy Slickback, the reality-TV-show host. This time, I thought I'd give him a home makeover show – with some unusual characters and an unexpected outcome. It's much like a "real" reality show you might see on TV.

Now, I wonder when they're coming round to my place to make everything ship-shape again!

Quentin Flynn
Author

Program Schedule

Coming Soon! Don't Miss It

Before and After

Featuring Soupy Slickback and the Grizzlethorpe Twins!

News and Weather 6.00 pm

Kids' Movies on Demand 7.30 pm

Channel 88: The best channel between 87 & 89!

1 Hoist the Mizzen!

"Weigh anchor and hoist the mizzen!" shouted the pirate captain. His leathery face was so close that Soupy Slickback, the world-famous TV-show host, could feel the pirate captain's sardine-scented breath on his quivering face.

"W-w-why do you want to know how heavy the anchor is?" he stammered. The TV-show host looked at his director for support, but she and the rest of the TV crew were cowering in a corner, surrounded by fearsome pirates armed with glinting cutlasses.

The pirate captain fixed Soupy Slickback with a bone-chilling look. "Ye useless landlubber," he snarled. "We're settin' sail for the South Seas, and if we hear another peep out of ye, ye'll be feeding the fishes."

The whimpering of the TV crew was drowned out by the blood-curdling growling and jeering of the pirates.

"B-b-but I don't have any fish food on me," pleaded Soupy Slickback.

A grim chuckle arose from the pirates.

"Aye, ye do!" growled the pirate captain. "We're talking big fishes, ye scurvy dog. Big fishes with mouthfuls of pointy, razor-sharp teeth! Ye *are* the fish food!"

"No, no, no," squealed Soupy in terror.

"Aye, aye, aye!" chanted the pirates, as they rattled and swished their cutlasses dangerously.

A murderous grin flashed across the pirate captain's face. "Shall we keelhaul him before we send him to Davey Jones's locker, mateys?" he asked, raising a perilous eyebrow at his crew.

"Aye, aye, aye!" they all shouted eagerly. The thought of tying a rope to the hapless TV-show host, tossing him in the water and dragging him beneath the ship sent shivers of gory delight up their salty spines.

"Shall we give him a taste of the cat-o'-nine-tails too?" added the pirate captain, licking his lips.

"Aye, aye, aye!" shouted the crew feverishly. They now had a taste for blood, and a whipping on the ship's deck was exactly the painful spectacle they craved. With renewed vigour, they rattled and swished their cutlasses wildly.

"Ouch!" yelped one of the pirates, looking in horror at the pinprick of blood welling up from his forefinger.

"Oops," muttered another apologetically. "Sorry, matey. I didn't mean to jab ye."

"What's the matter?" demanded the pirate captain.

"Cut!" said the wounded pirate, holding up his forefinger for all to see.

"CUT!" echoed the director, who was getting to her feet. "That's a wrap, folks," she added.

The pirate captain and his crew looked disappointed. Things aboard the fearsome pirate ship *Charybdis* were just getting interesting.

2 The Bad Ship *Charybdis*

TWO WEEKS EARLIER

"Pirating sure ain't what it used to be," grumbled Captain Grizzlethorpe, reaching for the TV remote control. The disgruntled crew of the *Charybdis* muttered and nodded their heads in resignation. Flotsam, the first mate, attempted a lacklustre ooh-arrgh, which turned into an embarrassing burp halfway through.

"Pardon me," he murmured.

The crew of the *Charybdis* had seen better days – and so had the cabin in which they sat. With its flickering TV screen, faded and moth-eaten comfortable chairs and half-eaten microwave dinners scattered around the deck, the *Charybdis* looked more like a weary retirement home for smelly buccaneers in need of a bath, than the fearsome scourge of the South Seas it had once been.

Jawbones, the second mate, wriggled around in his chair uncomfortably. He screwed up his face and spat a microwaved pea out from the gap in his front teeth.

"Vegetables," he frowned, with a disgusted look. "Whatever happened to the good ol' days when dinners were just brown?"

"Aye, and they had browner gravy to hide the bits that weren't brown enough," agreed Flotsam with a sigh. "They were the good ol' days."

The rest of the pirates harrumphed and aarghed and rustled their cutlasses feebly in agreement. It had been quite a few years since any of them had woken up to a good ol' day.

A piercing squeal suddenly cut through the fusty atmosphere of the cabin as Captain Grizzlethorpe fiddled with his hearing aid.

"Be quiet, ye scurvy dogs," he complained. "I'm trying to listen to the telly."

The harrumphing and ooh-arrghing died down as everyone peered towards the TV to see what had caught Captain Grizzlethorpe's attention.

A crackly voice filled the cabin. It was Soupy Slickback, world-famous reality-TV-show host.

"Welcome back, folks!" shouted Soupy from the TV screen. He grinned and the diamond filling in his front tooth sparkled.

"We're live, here at the Cooper family home. You're watching *Before and After*, the reality show where we give a complete makeover to one family's home in one hour! Remember, your phone votes will result in one of the family members receiving a complete style and wardrobe makeover, too!"

The camera panned away from Soupy Slickback and across a newly redecorated bedroom. In the corner, an excited teenager could barely contain herself. When Soupy pulled back a tarpaulin to reveal a wall covered with pink polka-dot wallpaper, the teenager burst into tears and started jabbering.

"Oh-my-goodness, oh-my-goodness, oh-my-goodness!" she wailed.

"I know just how that lass feels," sympathised Jawbones. "I feel like bawling me eyes out when I see a perfectly good dinner ruined with bits o' green."

"I like the wallpaper," said Flotsam, nodding his approval.

In his younger days, Captain Grizzlethorpe would have whirled around and silenced his pirate crew with a steely eye. Now, the crew was forced to wait patiently as he inched his threadbare armchair around in a series of clumps and bumps, accompanied by bursts of wheezing and muttered seafarer's curses.

"Any of you useless landlubbers know what an 'email' is?" he asked, flicking his eyes from pirate to pirate. "It says down the bottom of

News and Weather 6.00 pm

Kids' Movies on Demand 7.30 pm

All movies are rated KG (Kids' Guidance). Channel 88 recommends adults should not watch these movies unless supervised by a responsible kid at all times.

the screen that if ye want to be on the show, you should send Soupy an email."

"An email?" mused Jawbones. "Blow me down if it ain't one o' them strange-looking Australian birds."

"That's an emu," snorted Captain Grizzlethorpe derisively. "Besides, they can't fly, so how would you ever expect it to make it to Soupy Slickback's studio?"

"We could send him a parrot instead," suggested Flotsam helpfully. "We used to have one round here somewhere." He started jabbing old tinfoil microwave dinner trays with his rusty cutlass. "Ahoy, Percy! Percy-percy-percy!"

"There he is," pointed out one of the other pirates. "He's dead!"

Flotsam heaved himself out of his chair with a groan of protest, and shuffled over to where the other pirate was pointing.

"Nope," he said, prodding the object gingerly with his cutlass. "That's an old corncob." He bent down and peered closely at it. "And it's still got someone's tooth in it," he said.

"Vegetables," grumbled Jawbones, rubbing his chin. "Nothing good ever comes of 'em."

"I think Percy's down here somewhere," said Captain Grizzlethorpe, squirming from side to side and feeling between the cushions of his armchair. "He dropped off me shoulder a month or two ago, and I haven't gotten around to putting him back on his perch. Ah! Thar she blows!"

Captain Grizzlethorpe's fingers closed around something squishy and he pulled it out triumphantly. Then his face fell.

"Oh, shiver me timbers, that's not Percy," he said, sounding disappointed. "That's a dead rat."

Eventually the pirate crew found Percy. Fortunately the *Charybdis*'s parrot had not expired between the pirates' recliner cushions or beneath a blanket of gravy-encrusted tinfoil plates. Instead, he was fast asleep, perched on a coathanger in the captain's wardrobe.

Captain Grizzlethorpe sharpened a pencil with his cutlass and wrote a message to Soupy Slickback on the back of an old tissue. Then he rolled it up and attached it to a rather surprised Percy's leg.

"That should do it," declared the captain. He took the bewildered parrot up to the poop deck of the *Charybdis* and tossed the bird high up into the air.

Percy almost hit the grey, oily water before he remembered what his wings were for. With a disgruntled squawk, he unfurled his feathers and swooped off between the cranes and containers that lined the grimy dock where the *Charybdis* had been anchored for as long as anyone could remember.

This week featuring THE COOPER FAMILY!

Captain Grizzlethorpe surveyed the grimy industrial surroundings and sighed. Once upon a time, he would have been greeted by scenes of South Sea islands, dotted with palms and ringed by sandy white beaches.

"Pirating sure ain't what it used to be," he repeated to himself. He shook his head disconsolately and slowly creaked his way back below deck.

News and Weather 6.00 pm

Kids' Movies on Demand 7.30 pm

All movies are rated KG (Kids' Guidance). Channel 88 recommends adults should not watch these movies unless supervised by a responsible kid at all times.

3 Before and After!

After a month with no reply, Captain Grizzlethorpe was beginning to wonder if it wouldn't have been quicker to actually send an emu.

"Modern technology," he muttered. "Slower than sending a message in a bottle." He peeled back the lid of another microwave meal. "French Bakery Delights" said the packaging. Captain Grizzlethorpe peered inside. The soggy grey pastries looked like they had been run over by a French forklift.

Suddenly, there was an alarming clatter overhead, along with the sounds of footsteps edging their way over the timbers and ropes that littered the deck of the *Charybdis*. Captain Grizzlethorpe's eyes narrowed and a fierce look swept across his face. He felt for his cutlass and, in less than forty-five seconds, shuffled around to face his crew.

"Avast, me hearties!" he bellowed to the pirates, who were snoozing in their armchairs. "I fear the *Charybdis* is being boarded! All hands on deck!"

Flotsam, Jawbones and the rest of the pirates whirled into action – action that was cleverly disguised as several minutes of wheezing and groaning and trying to push themselves out of their armchairs. The clatter overhead turned into a thumping cascade of footsteps tumbling down the stepladder and approaching the cabin.

Jawbones, who had temporarily misplaced his cutlass, felt in his pockets for the old flintlock pistol he knew he kept around somewhere and drew it out threateningly.

"We're armed and dangerous!" he growled alarmingly. "Be prepared to meet the fish!"

A split second later, the cabin door burst open and the gloomy cabin was flooded with blinding white light. Captain Grizzlethorpe and the other pirates squinted in the dazzling glare.

"Ahoy there!" boomed a strangely familiar voice. "I'm Soupy Slickback and we're live, here at the Grizzlethorpe family home. You're watching

Before and After, the reality show where we give a complete makeover to one family's home in one hour! Remember, your phone votes will result in one of those family members receiving a complete style and wardrobe makeover, too!"

Soupy peered at Jawbones. "Why are you pointing a TV remote control at me?"

Jawbones's finger twitched over the trigger of what he thought was a flintlock pistol and, in the corner of the cabin, the TV flickered into life.

"Well, blow me down," he muttered, staring at what he'd been sure was a deadly weapon.

"Well, blow me down," came a crackly voice from the TV.

Captain Grizzlethorpe, Jawbones, Flotsam and the other pirates stared at the TV screen. It was filled with an image of what looked like dishevelled senior citizens in fancy dress, their whiskers full of dried microwave morsels and their slippered feet surrounded by corncobs and crumpled foil trays.

Then Soupy's face filled the screen and the diamond filling in his tooth sparkled.

"We'll be right back after this commercial break!" he beamed.

Two seconds later, a woman with a baseball cap with "Director" on it yelled out "Cut!" and unfolded a deck chair with a large gold star on it for Soupy Slickback.

"I've seen some run-down families and some run-down homes," said Soupy, whistling through his teeth, "but this one takes the cake. You know we've only got an hour to complete our *Before and After* makeover, not an entire season?"

"It's not so bad," protested Captain Grizzlethorpe, trying to stuff the dead rat back between the cushions of his recliner.

"And the program is supposed to be for families," said Soupy, eyeing the other pirates suspiciously. "You *are* a family, I suppose?"

The captain pondered his response for a few seconds. "Aye," he said slowly. "We're twins."

"What?" said Soupy. "All thirteen of you?"

"Aye, aye, aye," mumbled the crew together nervously. "Twins."

"Well, that's alright then," grinned Soupy.

He beckoned the director over. “Our director will get you to sign our contract, which states that we are able to redecorate your ... er, house ... however we like. Are all the participants in agreement?”

The pirates nodded.

“Can we have the pink polka-dot wallpaper?” asked Flotsam hopefully.

Soupy surveyed the cabin walls, which were already covered in polka dots of black mildew and splatters of unidentifiable microwave dinner sauce.

“Anything will be an improvement,” he said. “Now, who are the three ... er, twins ... that you want to nominate to compete for our complete style and wardrobe makeover?”

4 Ooh-Arrgh, Ooh-Arrgh

"Live in five ... four ... three ... two ...," called the director. She swept her hand around and pointed to Soupy Slickback on the silent count of "one".

"Welcome back, folks!" shouted Soupy to the TV camera. "We're live, here at the Grizzlethorpe family home. You're watching *Before and After*, the reality show where we give a complete makeover to one family's home in one hour! And this week, and this family, is going to be a challenge like no other!"

The camera panned across a row of nervous-looking pirates.

"Wave your cutlasses!" hissed the director, flapping her hand anxiously. "Like I told you."

"Ooh-arrgh, ooh-arrgh," went the pirates, jostling each other's elbows. Jawbones gave a toothless grin.

"Wicked!" said Soupy, flashing his trademark sparkling diamond tooth.

"I'd like to introduce you to the Grizzlethorpe twins," he continued. "A fine, upstanding family of honest seafarers who have fallen on hard times."

"Ooh-arrgh, ooh-arrgh," went Captain Grizzlethorpe again, for extra effect. The director rolled her eyes and drew a finger across her throat.

"Oops, sorry," mumbled Captain Grizzlethorpe, looking at his feet in embarrassment.

"Now, before we start the *Before and After* makeover on the good ship *Charybdis*, we're asking viewers to vote for which pirate they want to get the complete style and wardrobe makeover," continued Soupy Slickback. "By the looks of these characters, it's going to take almost as long to redecorate the poor fellows as it will to redecorate their ship!"

There was a moment's expectant silence. The director sighed peevishly and flapped her hand again.

"Ooh-arrgh, ooh-arrgh," went the pirates, remembering the instructions they had been given.

"Got your pens and paper ready, folks?" said Soupy, cocking his head and flashing a smile. He drew an envelope from his pocket. "And our first contender is ..." He paused for a second while the pirates jiggled from foot to foot in anticipation. "Flotsam!" boomed Soupy triumphantly.

Hands clasped to his face in delight, Flotsam squealed with excitement.

Captain Grizzlethorpe, who thought the squealing was coming from his hearing aid, fiddled with his earpiece.

"To vote for Flotsam, just call 0800-FLOTSAM. The *Before and After* voting lines are now open!" said Soupy, beaming at the camera. "And our next contender is ..."

Soupy pulled out another envelope. The director drew her finger across her throat once more and the pirates, following instructions, fell silent. Each pirate glanced nervously at the pirate next to him, their eyes swivelling like marbles rolling around dinner plates.

"Jawbones!" yelled Soupy. Jawbones started blubbering with thinly disguised relief and his toothless mouth opened and closed like a goldfish gulping for air.

"To vote for Jawbones, just call 0800-JAWBONE. You can transform this man's dreams into reality, ladies and gentlemen!" Soupy carried on.

"This means so much to me," sobbed Jawbones, hugging the surprised pirate next to him.

"And our final contender will be ..." Soupy reached into his pocket and held up the final envelope. His teeth flashed as he read the card inside. "Captain Grizzlethorpe!" he revealed to wild applause.

Captain Grizzlethorpe breathed a sigh of relief.

"Ooh-arrgh, ooh-arrgh," cheered the other pirates in unison.

"0800-GRIZZLE," said Soupy, pointing directly at the camera. "That's the number to call if you want to vote for Captain Grizzlethorpe. Now,

remember, ladies and gentlemen, you've only got a few minutes to vote while we take a commercial break, so get dialling right now!"

From behind the camera, the director started counting down on her fingers. Five ... four ... three ...

"And now it's time for some messages from our sponsors. We'll be getting started on our *Before and After* makeover when we come back – and we'll reveal which of our contenders you voted for!"

"And we're clear," confirmed the director. Soupy headed for the deck chair emblazoned with a gold star and the pirates headed for their moth-eaten armchairs.

"Me legs are killing me," wheezed Captain Grizzlethorpe as he wriggled around in his chair. "Who'd have thought being a reality TV star would be so exhausting?"

News and Weather 6.00 pm

Kids' Movies on Demand 7.30 pm

All movies are rated KG (Kids' Guidance). Channel 88 recommends adults should not watch these movies unless supervised by a responsible kid at all times.

5 The *Charybdis* Transformed

By the time the commercial break was over, the pirate ship *Charybdis* was swarming with interior designers, carpenters, painters, wallpaper decorators and carpet layers, all unfurling measuring tapes and shaking their heads while tut-tut-tutting.

The camera focused on the pirates.

"She'll be shipshape in no time," grunted Captain Grizzlethorpe from the comfort of his armchair.

"Ooh-arrgh, ooh-arrgh," nodded the other pirates.

"I hope they go for a French countryside shabby chic look," said Jawbones hopefully. "A little brocade and some nice net curtains and scatter cushions up in me crow's nest would make all the difference when I'm on lookout duty," he said. "Plain decking, braided rope borders and weathered timbers are so last century."

"Aye," agreed Flotsam thoughtfully. "But clean lines and bold use of contrasting pastels would make much more of a statement, don't you think? A minimalist look is much more me," he added, grinning a toothless grin at the camera.

"Aye," grumbled Captain Grizzlethorpe. "We can see by your teeth you've already been working on your minimalist look."

The camera operator pointed the camera at Soupy Slickback, who was looking at a piece of paper the director had handed him.

"And I've just been handed the results of our phone voting," Soupy announced. "In third place, with 54 000 votes is ... Flotsam! Flotsam, what do you think about that?"

"I'm just grateful that so many people think I need a makeover," said Flotsam graciously. "It's taken years to achieve this look, and I'm delighted to know all me hard work's paid off."

Soupy Slickback flashed his diamond tooth and looked back at the camera. "And the runner-up, with 67 000 votes is ... Jawbones!"

"It's all down to vegetables," declared Jawbones triumphantly. "I'd never have made it this far if I hadn't avoided them like the plague!"

Soupy Slickback wheeled around to face Captain Grizzlethorpe. "And our viewers are all dying to know what you're thinking right now, Captain."

"I'm wondering who won," said Captain Grizzlethorpe. "The suspense is killin' me."

"That's hilarious, Captain," said Soupy, slapping his thigh before realising that the captain wasn't joking. He cleared his throat. "With 104 000 votes, you're the lucky recipient of the *Before and After* style and wardrobe makeover!"

"Well, blow me down and shiver me timbers!" declared Captain Grizzlethorpe. "There's a surprise."

While Captain Grizzlethorpe was undergoing his style and wardrobe transformation in another cabin, the other pirates were amazed at the rapid progress the tradespeople were making on the transformation of the *Charybdis*.

"I had no idea there was such good timber decking underneath all that," said Flotsam in surprise, after the layer of crusty microwave trays had been swept off the main cabin deck. "A nice kilim will bring up the natural warmth of the timber beautifully, don't you agree, Jawbones?"

"Kill 'im?" repeated Jawbones, feeling for his cutlass. "Kill who?"

"Middle Eastern rugs," said Flotsam wearily. "They're called kilims."

Above decks, everything was scrubbed, sanded, painted and varnished. The contents of a truck laden with leather furniture, tapestries, imported wallpaper and shiny brass electrical fittings were carried up the gangplank and down into the main cabin.

From every angle, the camera operator filmed Soupy Slickback inspecting the progress.

"Will you have enough time?" Soupy asked a wallpaper decorator, who was hanging rolls of plum damask wallpaper in the cabin.

"It'll be tight," said the wallpaper decorator. "There's a lot to do in only sixty minutes."

"There sure is," agreed Soupy. He crouched down and spoke to a carpet layer, who was expertly installing a colourful floral Axminster carpet around the edges of the cabin.

"We're leaving the central area exposed," explained the carpet layer. "That beautiful timber will make a lovely dance floor," he said.

Soupy turned to a carpenter, who was busily constructing what looked like a large umbrella stand. "It's a cutlass rack," the carpenter explained. "With all the rattling and waving those poor pirates have to do, I could just tell they needed somewhere to keep their cutlasses."

Soupy was about to make a clever comment about the cutlasses when an angry roar reverberated through the *Charybdis*.

"What was that?" he said in alarm. There was another thundering roar. The camera operator followed Soupy as he headed in the direction of the noise, which was coming from the cabin where Captain Grizzlethorpe was receiving his style and wardrobe makeover.

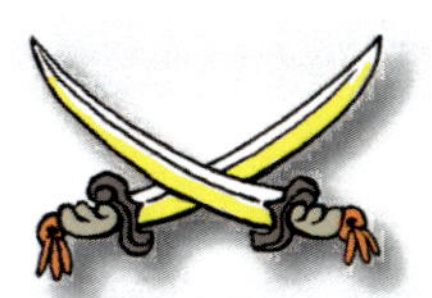

6 All Hands on Deck!

"What's going on?" asked Soupy, peering into the captain's cabin.

"I thought ye were going to make over me wardrobe," blustered Captain Grizzlethorpe.

"We are," said Soupy with a puzzled look.

"Well, me wardrobe's a square bit of furniture I keep in me cabin," retorted the captain. "It's got me clothes, and sometimes me parrot, in it. I thought ye'd be giving her a lick o' paint, that's all."

"No, we wanted to update your clothes," explained Soupy. "That's what we meant by a wardrobe makeover."

"There's nothing wrong with me clothes," snorted Captain Grizzlethorpe. "I've worn them for 37 years, even in the bath, and they don't need changing yet."

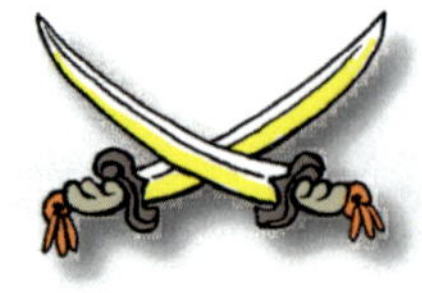

Back in the main cabin, the transformation was almost complete.

"Ooh-arrgh, ooh-arrgh," murmured the other pirates approvingly. Their cutlasses had been collected for refurbishing, so they waved their fists instead.

A glittering line of crystal lamps sparkled from the newly wallpapered walls. Beneath the plum damask wallpaper, panels of golden cherry wood completed a look of elegant sophistication. The floral Axminster carpet was fully installed, and painters were busily finishing the final coat of varnish to protect the freshly sanded floorboards.

"It's a pity they could only afford couches with one arm," said Jawbones.

"They're called *chaise longues*," whispered Flotsam. "They're supposed to be that way. You don't just sit in them. You're supposed to drape yourself languidly on them."

With much ooh-arrghing, the pirates practised draping themselves languidly on the chaise longues. Then they examined the fine china teacups, saucers and cake plates that adorned the nearby occasional tables.

"If ye only use 'em as tables occasionally," frowned Jawbones, "what do ye use 'em for the rest of the time?"

Flotsam wasn't sure. "Perhaps you tie them together and use them as a life raft if you have to abandon ship," he suggested. "Or maybe you stand on them to get a better view with a spyglass."

At one end of the cabin, the carpenters had built a buffet table, on which sat a cappuccino machine, a kettle that went "ping" when the water boiled and a polished cedar box full of all sorts of teabags.

Flotsam rustled through the teabags. "There's Assam, Darjeeling, Jasmine, Pure Ceylon and Oolong," he said.

"Is there any Ooh-arrgh-long?" guffawed Jawbones, much to the amusement of the other pirates. "Now that's what I'd call a real pirate tea!"

There was a loud clatter as one of the tradespeople dropped an armful of glinting, gleaming, refurbished cutlasses into the new cutlass rack. The pirate crew eagerly examined their sharp and shiny new cutlasses, and swished them proudly through the air. Suddenly Soupy Slickback and the camera crew burst into the cabin.

“Viewers, are you ready for the ‘reveal’?” he said excitedly. “What will Captain Grizzlethorpe’s crew think of their new captain? Will they even recognise him after he walks in that door?”

There was a commotion outside and Captain Grizzlethorpe’s raised voice could be heard grumbling.

“I said ye could brush me hair,” came his voice. “But I never said ye could comb the fish bones out of me nostrils! That’s a step too far, laddie!”

The director waved her hand in urgent circles, signalling to Soupy that he should hurry up.

“You’ve seen him before!” shouted Soupy, with a sweep of his arm. “Now you can see him after. Come on in, Captain Grizzlethorpe!”

Soupy clapped furiously, and the pirate crew rattled their refurbished cutlasses in gleeful accompaniment to a hearty chorus of oohing and arrghing. Captain Grizzlethorpe appeared in the doorway.

“The transformation is so natural, you’d hardly notice anything different!” said Soupy Slickback. “What do you think, viewers? Isn’t it all a huge surprise?”

“Aye, and this’ll be a huge surprise, too!” fumed the captain. He grabbed the remaining cutlass from the cutlass rack and lunged towards Soupy Slickback.

“Keep the camera rolling!” hissed the director under her breath. “This could make our ratings skyrocket!”

“Now, for the first time in too many years, we’re going PIRATING!” declared Captain Grizzlethorpe. “Weigh anchor and hoist the mizzen!” he shouted. His leathery face was so close that Soupy Slickback, the world-famous TV-show host, could feel the pirate captain’s sardine-scented breath on his quivering face.

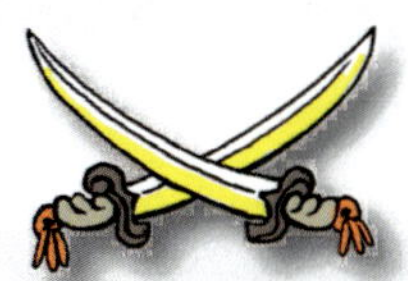

“Hoist the sails and set a course for the South Seas,” bellowed Captain Grizzlethorpe from behind his freshly polished and redecorated ship’s wheel.

"Aye, aye, Cap'n," chanted the pirates, as they heaved and hoed. The *Charybdis* slowly stirred from its moorings and started to drift away from the grimy wharf where it had lain for years.

"Cap'n!" said Flotsam, the first mate. "Can ye just remind us where exactly the South Seas are? It's been a while, ye know, and me navigational skills are a bit rusty."

"That way," replied Captain Grizzlethorpe, pointing his shiny refurbished cutlass into the wind. "And send Jawbones up into the crow's nest to keep an eye out for any vessels along the way. This captain's in the mood for some pirating," he added with an evil chuckle.

"Ooh-arrgh, ooh-arrgh," cheered the other pirates. "Pirating!"

"Are we allowed to show pillaging and plundering on *Before and After*?" whispered Soupy to the director. "We *are* supposed to be a family show." Before the *Charybdis* had set sail, the tradespeople had been sent down the gangplank – and Soupy and the crew of *Before and After* had been brought above decks. They were made to sit next to an ominous plank jutting out over the water lapping below.

"Shh," said the director. She whistled at the camera operator. "Are we still live?"

"We're live," confirmed the camera operator. He looked nervously at the plank. "For now."

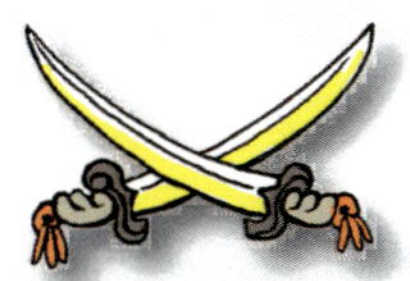

The breeze picked up and the *Charybdis*'s sails billowed. The pirate ship headed south and after barely a minute, there was an excited shout from the crow's nest.

"Ahoy, there, Cap'n," called Jawbones. "A galleon to the starboard. Well, more of a pleasure yacht, really."

"Take her starboard!" commanded Captain Grizzlethorpe, as he spun the ship's wheel around.

"And Cap'n!" shouted Jawbones.

"What?" replied Captain Grizzlethorpe.

"Can ye tell Soupy that I love me net curtains and scatter cushions. Very me."

The *Charybdis* bore down on the pleasure yacht at a clipping pace. Her unsuspecting crew had no idea of the terrible fate about to befall them. At the last minute, Captain Grizzlethorpe swung the ship's wheel around and the *Charybdis* drew parallel with its prey. The pirates swung grappling hooks wildly and, to their surprise, one or two of them even landed on the pleasure yacht's railing.

"Ahoy, me hearties!" bellowed the captain. "Prepare to board!"

"Are you getting this?" said the director to the camera operator.

"Aye, aye," replied the camera operator. "I mean, yes. Sorry. Got caught up in the moment."

Captain Grizzlethorpe held the *Charybdis* steady and, within seconds, the pirate crew swarmed aboard the pleasure yacht.

"Pan to Soupy," hissed the director. The camera operator swung his camera around to Soupy's nervous face, while the director started counting down on her fingers. Five ... four ... three ...

"W-w-we'll be right back after this commercial break," stammered Soupy.

Captain Grizzlethorpe draped himself languidly over one of the chaise longues. The sound of fine china gently clinking and chinking filled the cabin below decks on the *Charybdis*.

"One lump or two?" he asked politely, as he handed a teacup and saucer to one of his captives. The crew of the pleasure yacht sat on one of the other chaise longues. There was an ominous gurgling sound from one end of the cabin.

"The milk's just frothing now," called out Jawbones from where he was operating the cappuccino machine. "Would you like low-fat or calcium-free?"

"How civilised," smiled one of the lady captives. "And I love what you've done to the place."

"We like it," replied Captain Grizzlethorpe, making sure to straighten his little finger before sipping his cup of Darjeeling. "And may I say how nice it is to have visitors. We hardly get anyone over for high tea these days, do we, lads?"

"Ooh-arrgh, ooh-arrgh," said the other pirates, shaking their heads. "A life upon the waves ain't what it used to be."

"Cucumber sandwich?" offered Flotsam, passing around the china cake stand. "Sliced them freshly myself," he added, flourishing his cutlass.

"I must say, we were a teeny bit worried when you surprised us like that," said the lady. "Seeing all of you naughty pirates, we rather feared ..."

"Ho ho," said Captain Grizzlethorpe. "That's only in films and on the telly. This is real life. We only wanted to show off the new spick-and-span *Charybdis* to some fellow seafarers."

"Besides," said Flotsam, "that was before. This is after. We're getting a bit old for all that plundering and pillaging stuff. It would be a bit undignified at our age, wouldn't it?" he smiled.

From the corner of the cabin, the director started counting down on her fingers. Five ... four ... three ...

"And that's it from this episode of *Before and After*," grinned Soupy Slickback, his trademark diamond tooth glinting in the light. "Or maybe we should call this nautical episode *Fore and Aft*," he winked. "We hope you enjoyed the show and we'll look forward to seeing you next week!"

"Cut!" called the director. Thirteen pirates drew their cutlasses and stood with their gleaming blades at the ready.

"Cut what?" they bellowed.

"No, no," explained Soupy. "She just means we're off the air."

"Oops, sorry," mumbled Captain Grizzlethorpe, putting his cutlass away. He sipped his Darjeeling. "Pirating sure ain't what it used to be," he added happily, reaching for another cucumber sandwich.

"It sure ain't," chimed in Soupy Slickback.

"And neither is the good ship *Charybdis*," he added with a sparkle of his tooth.

The merry crew of the pirate ship gave a hearty "aye-aye", and clinked their cups and saucers in genteel agreement. Flotsam attempted a jolly ooh-arrgh, which turned into an embarrassing burp halfway through.

"Pardon me," he murmured.

Captain Grizzlethorpe winked at Soupy. "But it seems some things never change. Before *or* after."